Sarah and the Barking Dog

Story by Jenny Giles

Illustrations by Priscilla Cutter

Sarah walked slowly
along the path to school.
She could see Kiran
waiting with her little sister.
But Sarah stopped
when she came to the white fence.
The big dog had seen her.

2

He jumped at the fence
and barked and barked.
Sarah started to run.
She ran and ran
as fast as she could
to Kiran's house.

After school, Mom and Lucy
came to meet Sarah.
"Here we are," called Mom.

"Oh, good," said Sarah.
"Now I don't have to walk
  past that big dog all by myself.
  It barks at me every day, Mom,
  and I'm scared of it."

"Look, Sarah," said Mom.
"The dog can't get you.
  It can't get over that tall fence,
  and the gate is always shut."

  Lucy looked into the garden.
"Hello, dog!" she called. "Hello, dog!"

Beware of the dog

"Don't say that, Lucy," cried Sarah.
"Don't wake him up!
We have to get home.
Come on!"

"Goodbye, dog," said Lucy.

The next morning,
Sarah tiptoed past the white fence,
but the dog saw her.

Grrr! Grrr! he went.
He ran to the gate
and jumped up.

Beware
of the dog

8

Woof! Woof! Woof! he barked,
and the gate rattled.

Sarah ran and ran to Kiran's house.
Her legs were still shaking
as she walked into the school.

That afternoon,
Sarah walked home
with Mom and Lucy again.

When they came to the house
where the big dog lived,
Sarah stopped.

"Look, Mom!" she said.
"There is a big truck
  in the drive!"

"So there is!" said Mom.
"The family must be moving away."

They all stopped and watched
as the truck drove slowly
past the gate
and down the road.

Then Sarah saw a car
following the truck.
Sitting up in the back of the car
was the big dog!
Lucy waved. "Hello, dog!" she said.

Sarah watched the car
as it drove away
down the road.

"Goodbye, dog!" called Lucy.

"Goodbye, dog!" laughed Sarah.
"Goodbye forever!"
Then she skipped past
the white fence
and all the way home.